The house looked deserted. But it wasn't, because I could hear music from inside. All the curtains were closed. Then, in a downstairs window, a curtain shivered – I was sure of it. It wasn't the only thing shivering, I can tell you. If I'd had any sense at all I'd have just run for it. But for some reason I didn't.

A thrilling story from Michael Morpurgo, award-winning author of *The Butterfly Lion* and *The Wreck of the Zanzibar*.

YOUNG CORGI BOOKS

Young Corgi books are perfect when you are looking for great books to read on your own. They are full of exciting stories and entertaining pictures and can be tackled with confidence. There are funny books, scary books, spine-tingling stories and mysterious ones. Whatever your interests you'll find something in Young Corgi to suit you: from ponies to football, from families to ghosts. The books are written by some of the most famous and popular of today's children's authors, and by some of the best new talents, too.

Whether you read one chapter a night, or devour the whole book in one sitting, you'll love Young Corgi – books to get your teeth into!

BLACK QUEEN

For dear Léa

BLACK QUEEN
A YOUNG CORGI BOOK : 0 552 546453

PRINTING HISTORY
Young Corgi edition published 2000

3 5 7 9 10 8 6 4 2

Copyright © Michael Morpurgo, 2000
Illustrations copyright © Tony Ross, 2000

Set in 16/20pt Bembo Schoolbook by
Phoenix Typesetting, Ilkley, West Yorkshire

Young Corgi Books are published by Transworld Publishers,
61–63 Uxbridge Road, Ealing, London W5 5SA,
a division of The Random House Group Ltd,
in Australia by Random House Australia (Pty) Ltd,
20 Alfred Street, Milsons Point, Sydney, NSW 2061, Australia,
in New Zealand by Random House New Zealand Ltd,
18 Poland Road, Glenfield, Auckland 10, New Zealand
and in South Africa by Random House (Pty) Ltd,
Endulini, 5a Jubilee Road, Parktown 2193, South Africa.

Made and printed in Great Britain by
Cox & Wyman Ltd, Reading, Berkshire

MICHAEL MORPURGO

Black Queen

Illustrated by Tony Ross

Chapter One

Matey Goes Missing

Of all the houses in all the streets, we have to move into Number 23, Victoria Gardens. Number 24 would have been fine; but no, we had to end up in Number 23, right next door to Number 22, and trouble, real trouble.

To begin with everything seemed perfect. On the outside Number 23 may have looked a bit old, a bit ramshackle; but as my mother said the day we moved in – and we all agreed – it was a house just made for us, a dream house.

For the first time in my life I didn't have to share a room with Rula – my little sister, six and sweet sometimes. We now had all the space we hadn't had back in the fourth-floor flat we'd come from. My father had his own den for his train set. (He's crazy about trains.) And we could leave the chess set out safely, in mid-game. (We all love chess in our family, even Rula.) My mother too had her own room at the top of the house for her painting. (She's crazy about painting, and reading – she loves reading.) We even had a basement room for Gran, so she could have some peace and quiet when she came to stay. But, best of all, we had a garden, a great big garden with a huge apple tree you could climb into, a goldfish pond with three goldfish, and a garden shed.

This garden shed at once became my own private hideaway, good for skulking in or sulking in, good for just being alone. Rula hated the place. (I made sure she did. I told her there were spiders in there, and there were too, lots of them, and all of them huge and horrible and hairy.) So she always left me alone in my shed, which was what I wanted. I was really happy. I had a new house, almost like a new life, and the whole summer holidays stretching away in front of me. And Rula was happy too. She had Matey.

Matey was Rula's oversized lop-eared grey rabbit with a white bobtail, and she was completely besotted with him. As for Matey, he must have thought he had arrived in bunny paradise. Back in the flat he had been stuck inside his smelly old hutch in the utility room, next to the washing machine. He'd never even seen grass before, only carpets. Now he had the entire garden to roam in. He could nibble all the grass he wanted, dig holes

in the flower beds and hop about like proper rabbits do. Rula would spend all her time in the garden hopping about on all fours with Matey. It takes all sorts, I suppose. Anyway, she was hopping happy; the whole house was happy – until the morning, a week or so after we had moved in, when Matey disappeared.

The two of them were playing out in the garden as usual, when Rula came running in for a drink. When she went back out again Matey just wasn't there. He had gone, vanished into thin air. We searched the garden first, then the house, from top to bottom, every nook and cranny. He was nowhere. Rula kept wailing over and over again: "I'll never see him again. I know I won't."

Nothing and no-one could stop her crying.

I decided I would go out into the garden again to have one last look, and my father came with me. That was when he discovered the hole under the fence right at the bottom of the garden behind my shed. It looked as if it had been freshly dug. We scrambled up and looked over the fence towards the garden of Number 24 to see if Matey had gone that way. Mrs Watson – we'd met her the day we moved in – was

outside in her fluffy green slippers hanging out her washing. No, she said, taking the clothes pegs out of her mouth, no, she hadn't seen a rabbit, but she'd certainly tell us if she did.

So we looked over the fence into the garden of Number 22. No sign of Matey there either. Mind you, it would have been rather difficult to spot him anyway in the garden of Number 22, because it was completely overgrown. The place was like a jungle. All I could see was a beehive, with lots of bees buzzing about, a tumble-down garden shed, a rusty roller up against the fence and a black cat sitting on top of a sundial, watching me with orange eyes.

I was all for climbing over there and then to see if I could find Matey, but my father held me back. We knew there was a Mrs Blume living in Number 22 – Mrs Watson had told us that much – but we hadn't even seen her yet, let alone met her. "We can't just go barging in, Billy," my father said. "We'd better ask first. Someone'll have to go round to the front door."

"I will," I said. I don't know why I volunteered, but I did.

So that was how I found myself going up the steps into the porch of Number 22 that afternoon. It was strange, but somehow I knew even then that once I had pressed that bell I would be starting something I would not be able to stop. I wasn't frightened exactly, but I was nervous, I admit it. But I could still hear Rula crying. I had no choice. I couldn't chicken out, not now.

I heard the bell echoing through the house. I waited, but no-one came. I rang again. Still no-one. I stepped back out of the porch, down a step or two, and looked up. The house looked deserted. But it wasn't, because I could hear music from inside. All the curtains were closed.

Then, in a downstairs window, a curtain shivered – I was sure of it. It wasn't the only thing shivering, I can tell you. If I'd had any sense at all I'd have just run for it. But for some reason I didn't. I heard footsteps. I saw a shadow looming closer behind the frosted glass door. I heard bolts grinding back, a key turning in the lock. Slowly, horribly slowly, the door opened.

Chapter 2

Black Queen

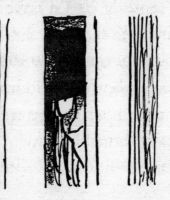

"Well?" It was a strange voice, deep and croaky, like no voice I'd heard before. The door had opened only a crack. She wore glasses – that was all I could see of her. "Well, what do you want?"

"I live next door," I began. My mouth was so dry I could hardly speak. "I just moved in."

"And?"

"It's our . . . We wondered if we could climb over into your garden. We lost our—"

"Football, right?" She sounded American, I thought, and not at all friendly.

"No," I said. "It's a rabbit."

"A rabbit! You mean to tell me you've got a rabbit that jumped right over the fence into my backyard? That's some rabbit." And the croak turned suddenly into a high-pitched chuckle. "What did he do? Pole-vault over? Trampoline? What?"

As I tried to explain how Matey had tunnelled his way out, the door opened a little wider, just enough for me to be able to see more of her. She seemed to be dressed entirely in a black coat of some kind, and she wore a floppy black hat with a wide brim that shaded her face. But I could see her eyes clearly through her glasses. They were darting about nervously all the time we spoke, at one moment fixing me with a piercing stare, the next looking out beyond me into the street.

She suddenly seemed in a hurry to get rid of me. "OK, OK," she said, the door closing again. "Listen, I don't want you snooping about in my backyard. Not you, not anyone. I'll go look for the rabbit myself, OK? Now, go on home. Get out of here."

I backed away down the steps, and was already out of the gate and in the

street when she called me back. "Hey, kid." She had the door open wider again. "I didn't mean to get mad at you. It's the bees. I wouldn't want you coming into my backyard on account of the bees. Those bees can be real mean.

And if they don't get you, then that grouchy old pussy cat of mine surely will. Rambo doesn't take kindly to strangers. Bit like me, I guess. Listen, kid, if I find that rabbit of yours, I'll let you know – that's a promise." The door closed.

I went on home. I just didn't know what to make of her. One minute she was frightening me half to death, the next laughing herself silly. One moment kind, the next moment nasty.

We were busy all the rest of that day putting up LOST RABBIT notices on every lamp post, in every shop window, at every bus stop, with our telephone number to call if anyone found him. But no-one called. We asked up and down the street, everywhere, but no-one had seen Matey.

That evening at supper, whilst everyone else was being sad about Matey, I couldn't stop myself talking about the lady in black at Number 22. "She was weird, really weird," I told them. "All in black, like that woman in the Addams family on the telly, in the cartoons – you know, that family of ghosts in the spooky house."

"Black Queen," my father said suddenly. "Her real name's Mrs Blume, of course, but everyone round here calls her the Black Queen – that's according to Mrs Watson next door. Loves to talk, does Mrs Watson. She told me all the gossip. Apparently that Mrs Blume hasn't been there long, just rents the place. A bit snooty, Mrs Watson says, a bit stand-offish. Always dresses in black – big long coat, big black hat. Never talks to anyone. She goes out walking on the common, but only at night. You hardly ever see her out by day."

"Like bats," I quipped. "Like vampires, like witches. She's got a black cat too. A witch! Maybe she's a real witch."

At that Rula began to cry all over again, into her baked beans. My mother eyed us both darkly as she tried to hug Rula better.

We both did our very best to put

things right. "Don't you worry, Roo," my father said sheepishly. "Matey'll be all right."

"He's just gone off to explore, probably," I added. "He'll be back tomorrow. You'll see." But neither of us really believed it and nor did Rula. She buried her head in my mother's arms and sobbed her heart out.

Chapter 3

Rabbit Stew

By lunchtime the next day there was still no sign of Matey. I was alone in the house. Everyone else was out. They had all gone shopping to cheer Rula up – Rula adores shopping. The chain had come off my bike again, and I was trying to mend it out in the garden, when I heard a voice.

"Hey, you! Hey, kid!" It was her! Mrs Blume! The Black Queen! She was peering over the fence at me in her floppy black hat, and smiling. Then, like a magician, she produced a rabbit – Matey – holding him up by the scruff of his neck and dangling him over the fence at me. "This your bunny rabbit?" she asked. "You want him?"

I was just tall enough to reach up and take him. "Where d'you find him?" I asked, cradling Matey in my arms.

"He was just sitting there in the grass. Rambo was eyeballing him. I reckon he was freaking him out, hypnotizing him. Hey, don't worry. No harm done. He's fine, just fine."

"Thanks," I said, setting Matey down on the grass. "Thanks a lot."

"I'm telling you, that's one fine rabbit you've got there. You take good care of him, you hear me. You don't want him ending up as rabbit stew, do you?"

And I heard her chuckling as she walked away, rustling through the long grass as she went. It was odd. I had met her twice now, and I still had no idea what she really looked like under that great floppy hat. She had long black hair – I had noticed that much. But why did she wear that hat inside the house as well as outside? And why was she always dressed in black as if she'd just been to a funeral?

By the time everyone came back I was sitting on the sofa with Matey lying beside me, his legs in the air – he loved having his tummy tickled. Rula hugged Matey half to death, and then she did the same to me. I told them it was the Black Queen who had found him, not me, but Rula kept on kissing me and hugging me and telling me I was the best brother ever, and at tea I got a double helping of ice-cream. It was good being a hero. I enjoyed it.

Later Rula was upstairs shrieking with joy in her bath. We all thought Matey was safely shut up in his hutch. I was filling in the hole under the fence –

my mother's idea – so that Matey couldn't escape again. I don't know what made me look. Just plain curiosity, I suppose. I scrambled up the fence and peered over into the Black Queen's garden. Rambo was sitting on the sundial, his tail swishing. His gaze was fixed on something in the long grass near the beehive. Matey! I could just make out the white of his bobtail in the grass. Somehow, he'd got out – again.

Number 22 looked dark. No lights on, the curtains closed. No music. Not a sign of anyone. Perhaps the Black Queen was out. I didn't much want to go over into her garden, not after what she'd told me about Rambo, about the bees. And she'd made it fairly obvious she didn't like being bothered, so I didn't want to go knocking on her door again either. I didn't know what to do. Suddenly Rambo sprang down off the sundial. I watched him snaking his way

through the grass towards Matey. I
wasn't sure whether or not cats can kill
rabbits, but I wasn't going to wait to find
out. I shinned up over the fence, let
myself down on the other side, and
hurdled through the long grass, keeping
as low as I could.

When Rambo saw me coming he
arched his back and turned his tail
instantly into a bottle brush. He didn't
run off, but stood his ground and hissed
at me furiously.

Matey was sitting in the grass, either rigid with fear or completely hypnotized – I didn't know which. I was aware now of the bees humming about me. I'd be as quick as I could. I crouched down, and was just about to pick up Matey when one of them landed on the back of my hand and stung me.

I was sitting there some moments later rocking back and forth in pain and nursing my throbbing hand, when I felt a shadow pass over me. I looked up. My blood ran cold. The Black Queen was looking down at me from out of the sun. Then she was helping me to my feet. "He stung you, right?" she said. "I did warn you, didn't I? I'm telling you, these bees are mean, real mean."

She was examining my hand now, and for the first time I could see her face properly. She was a lot younger than I

29

had thought. Not old at all, more middle-aged.

From her voice and from her clothes I had imagined her to be much, much older. The floppy hat looked as if it was made of velvet, the coat too.

"Come in the house," she said. "I'll fix up that bee sting for you. You'd better bring that bunny rabbit along with you." I must have looked as reluctant as I felt. "Look, kid, I'm not going to eat you. And I'm not going to eat the rabbit either. I never did like rabbit stew."

So, carrying Matey with me, I found myself following the Black Queen up the steps into the darkness of the house. All the time I was thinking: I shouldn't be doing this, this is silly. But somehow I couldn't seem to stop myself. It was almost as if I was being led up the steps by some unseen hand, as if I was under some kind of magical spell.

Chapter 4

Fixed Up

The house smelt of coffee – that was the first thing I noticed. She didn't say much, not to start with. She led me into the kitchen, and sat me down at the table. She filled a bowl with cold water, dropped in dozens of ice cubes, took my hand and plunged it in. Then she turned on the CD player, and the room filled with music.

"You've got to keep it there," she said. "It'll stop it swelling up. The music'll help. Music always helps everything. You want a Coke?"

The Coke was ice-cold too.
Everything was tidy and in its place –
not at all like home – almost as if the
place wasn't lived in at all. Then I saw
the chessboards. They were everywhere,
hung on the walls like pictures, propped
up on the sideboard. Just chessboards,
nothing else. Each of them was different
– marbles ones, wooden ones, all sorts.
There were no pieces, no kings, no
queens, no knights, no castles, just the
boards. It was weird, really weird.

"My son's," she said, "they're all my
son's. He collects them. I guess you could
say he's a kind of chess nut. Not a
walnut but a chestnut." She stifled a little
chuckle, but it was a few moments
before I saw the joke. "Do you play?"
she went on.

"We all do," I told her. "My father
really likes it. He says it's the best game
in the world – good for the brain, helps
you to think, he says. I can beat Rula

and Mum every time. Never beaten
Dad though."

"So you're a bit of a chess nut too
then," she said, smiling at me. "You got a
name?" she went on.

"Billy."

"Billy the Kid," she laughed, and I
laughed with her. I was beginning to
like her. She asked all sorts of questions
about me and my family, about where
we'd come from, what school I went to;

and all the time I felt her eyes on me, as if she was reading me like a book. From time to time she'd have a quick look to see how my hand was doing. "I hate those lousy bees," she said. "Nothing to do with me. They kind of came with the property. I only rent the place. I've asked a dozen times for them to be taken away but no-one seems to want to do it. Still, at least you zapped one of them for me. They die, you know. If a bee stings you, it dies. Did you know that?"

I didn't. By the time the Black Queen lifted my hand out of the water a while later, I think she knew just about all there was to know about me. But I still knew very little, if anything, about her.

"There," she said, giving me back my hand. "It looks all fixed up to me." And it was too. There was hardly a mark left, and all the pain had gone. It was amazing.

We were on our way out of the house when I felt her hand on my shoulder. "Billy," she said, "I've been thinking. You could be the answer to my prayers. You want to help me out? It's no big deal, honest. The thing is: the day after tomorrow I have to go back home to America for a while, to New York, just for a couple of weeks. I have to see my son, the chess one. I have to go to visit him; but I can't, not unless I find someone to cat-sit Rambo."

"Cat-sit?"

"Feed him, keep an eye out for him. That sort of thing. Would you do it for me? I guess I could put him in the cat home, but I wouldn't feel right about it. He'd just hate being all shut up like that. He'd curl up and die, I know he would."

"OK," I said. If I was thinking at all when I said it, I suppose I must have been thinking that one good turn deserves another. All I know is that I had no idea what I was letting myself in for. I was about to find that out.

"You're a real nice kid, Billy," she said, as we went down the steps into the garden. "But there's a little problem. Like I told you, Rambo doesn't take too kindly to strangers. He's kind of wild, I guess. The only person in the entire world he gets on with is me. I mean, he's sort of real fixated on me. Hates everyone else, loves me. So if you're going to feed him for me, you've got to pretend to be me, else he'll just run off some place, and then of course he won't have anything to eat at all. So, Billy, do you think you could do that?"

"How do you mean?" I asked.

"Well," she said, "I guess you've just got to sound like me a little. And of course you've got to look like me too."

"You mean I've got to dress up? Like you?" I simply could not believe what I was being asked to do.

"Well, it worked just fine before. I had a friend who came over a while back, when I was real sick. I had the flu pretty bad. He just put on my hat and my glasses and my coat and then he called him just like I do. Rambo never knew the difference. Came running for it, sweet as pie."

"I don't know," I said. "I'm not sure."

"You'll do just fine," she went on. "Just once a day for a few days, a couple of weeks. What d'you say?"

I was in so far now that I didn't know how to get out. "All right," I said, weakly.

She ruffled my hair. "I knew you were a great kid. I saw it in your eyes, first time I met you – that's the kind of kid I can trust, I thought. I've only got to look in a person's eyes and I know just what they're thinking, just what they're going to do next." Now she was being scary again. "But the thing is, Billy," she went on, lowering her voice confidentially, "I don't want anyone in the neighbourhood to know I've gone, that you're feeding my cat for me. If word gets about a place is empty, you

can get burglarized, vandalized. So
you'll be the only neighbour who'll
know I'm not here. No-one else, right?
You hear what I'm saying? Best if you
say nothing to nobody, right? Our little
secret."

I nodded.

"Promise me then?"

"I promise," I said, and at once wished
I hadn't. Desperately, I sought for a way
out, a way not to have to do it, any of it.
"What about the cat food? What about
the clothes?"

We were outside in the
garden by now. She
crouched down
and lifted up an
empty flower pot
by the sundial.
"I'll leave the key
right here, Billy.
How'll that be?
Then you can let

yourself in. I'll leave out his bowl and all the cat food you'll need on the kitchen table, and a can opener with it. There'll be some milk left in the ice-box. When it's finished you can give him water instead. He'll be fine. I've got an old hat and coat that'll do the trick. I'll leave them in the kitchen for you, OK? I feed him right here. You just come down these steps tap-tapping away at his bowl with a spoon, and calling him like this: 'Rammy Rambo! Rammy Rambo!' He'll come, no problem. But don't ever let him inside the house, OK? First off, he loves it in there, you'd never get him out again. Second, he tears my curtains to pieces with his claws; and third, he makes messes – if you get my meaning."

I did. But the cat seemed the least of my worries as I ran down the garden to climb back over. I just wanted to get away before she asked me to do anything more. Already I had promised to keep a secret I didn't want to keep, dress up like some mad old witch, *and* feed a cat that I didn't like the look of, not one bit.

"Hey, Billy," she called after me, "aren't you forgetting something?"

For a moment I had no idea what she was talking about. Then I saw Matey hopping towards me through the long grass. I bent to pick him up.

She was chuckling. "The day after tomorrow, Billy. Don't you go forgetting now."

Forget? I only wished I could.

Chapter 5

Sometimes It's Hard to Be a Woman

I lay in bed that night quite unable to sleep. The more I thought about it the worse it became – everything I had let myself in for. And what about the Black Queen herself? Who on earth was she? What was she? I just couldn't get it out of my head that she really might be some kind of witch. She certainly had powers. Hadn't she healed my bee sting? Hadn't she bewitched me into promising to do all sorts of things I didn't want to? At best she was strange; at worst . . . it made me shiver to think of it.

All the next day I kept thinking that I should tell my mother all about her, about what the Black Queen had asked me to do. But I said nothing. To be honest, it wasn't because I had promised to keep quiet about it; it was because I had it in my mind – and I know it sounds silly – that the Black Queen might do something terrible to me if she ever found out. Maybe she'd turn me into a bee. Maybe all those bees were spellbound spirits she had punished, condemning them to live out their days in the beehive at the bottom of her garden. My mind was in a constant whirl of terror. I longed to tell all, and that evening I very nearly did too.

After supper I was playing chess with my father. Rula was watching and fidgeting as usual. I just couldn't concentrate, but it wasn't Rula's fault. Every time I looked at the black queen on the chessboard my mind drifted back

to Number 22. I kept wondering why
there should be so many chessboards
there. And why have boards without the
pieces? Could they be part of some
mysterious and dreadful witch's rite?

My father had me checkmate in ten
minutes.

"You're miles away, Billy," he said.
"Anything the matter? You don't look
too good."

I should have spoken up. I had the chance, but I didn't. "Not in the mood," I said, and left it at that.

I had another sleepless night, thinking how hard it was going to be to pretend to be a woman, dreading everything I had to do the next day. I drifted in and out of nightmarish dreams – dreams full of killer bees and haunted houses and cackling witches, and a prowling black jaguar with orange eyes which chased me through the jungle.

By the next morning I really did not want to go and feed Rambo at all. I kept trying to convince myself that promises didn't matter. Rambo could manage by himself – he'd catch a few mice, he'd murder a few robins. He didn't need me to feed him, he'd be fine. But when I went out into the garden and heard him yowling pitifully on the other side of the fence, I knew I couldn't just leave him to starve. I had to do it, I had no choice.

My father was out at work, and the others had gone shopping. It was now or never. I scrambled over the fence and dropped down into the long grass the other side. Rambo hissed horribly at me from the top of the sundial. He even swiped his claws at me as I crouched down to see if the key was under the flower pot, where the Black Queen had said it would be. It was.

Quick as a flash I was up the steps and inside the house. My heart was pounding in my ears. I wanted to get it all over as quickly as possible. The black coat and the floppy black hat were ready and waiting. She'd left some glasses too. I put them on and got dressed up. I opened a tin of cat food and scooped it out into the bowl, all the while trying to remember how exactly

she had called for Rambo. I practised
out loud in the kitchen, imitating her
accent, her tone of voice. "Rammy
Rambo!" I called out. "Rammy
Rambo!" It didn't sound at all
convincing to me.

I was just making my way out of the
kitchen into the hallway, the bowl and
spoon at the ready, when I remembered
the milk. I went back to the fridge to get
it, took out a bottle and nudged the
door shut. I was all set. As I came out
into the hallway again I was still
practising my "Rammy Rambo" call out
loud. I was getting better at it all the
time. I had the bowl in one hand, the
milk bottle in the other. That was the
moment I heard someone coughing.

It sounded at first as if there was
someone in the house. A chill of fear
crept up my spine. Then I saw the
shadow outside the front door, through
the frosted glass. I froze where I stood

and held my breath. How the milk bottle slipped out of my hand I do not know, but the crash of it echoed through the empty house, echoes that seemed to go on for ever.

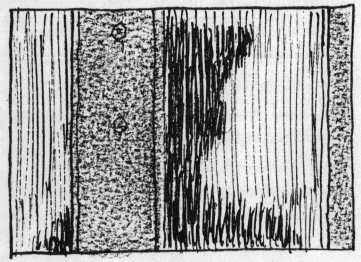

"Are you all right in there, Mrs Blume?" The milkman! I knew his voice. "I thought you said you were away for a couple of weeks."

He could see me through the glass. I couldn't just stand there. I had to say something. "Tomorrow. I'm off tomorrow," I called out, in her voice, in

her accent. "A little accident, that's all."
I could see his face was pressed up
against the glass. "I'm fine, just fine."

There was a long pause.

"You sure you're all right?"

"I'm sure. Thanks anyway."

There was a long silence; then the
shadow bent down. "OK then. I'll just
pick up the empties. Have a good trip."

I heard the clinking of bottles and
then his footsteps going away down the
steps. I couldn't believe it. I had got
away with it! I had fooled him! It was
all I could do to stop myself giggling
with triumph as I swept up the glass and
mopped up the milk. I could hear
Rambo yowling out in the garden. If I
can fool the milkman, I thought, then I
can fool Rambo. He was only a cat,
after all.

I did just as the Black Queen had told
me. Tapping the bowl, I went down the
steps into the garden and called out:

"Rammy Rambo! Rammy Rambo!"
Sure enough, Rambo came at once,
springing down off the sundial and
bounding up the steps to meet me. He
purred as he ate, his tail trembling with
pleasure. It worked! So far as Rambo
was concerned I *was* Mrs Blume, I *was*
the Black Queen. I even felt confident
enough to stroke him, and he didn't

seem to mind at all. I went
back into the house and
fetched another bottle of
milk. I poured it out for
him and crouched down
to watch him lap at it,
dipping his pink tongue in
and out so delicately.

Then, a sudden movement out of the
corner of my eye! Rula! Rula was
peering at me over the garden fence. All
I could see of her were two little hands
and a round red face. Her eyes were
wide with fear.

I knew then that this was the moment of truth. "Hi there," I called out as breezily as I could. I sounded just like the Black Queen. It was amazing. "Just feeding my pussy cat. You got a pussy cat?"

Rula couldn't seem to find her voice for a moment or two – which was unusual for her. "I've got a rabbit," she said at last.

"A real live bunny rabbit?" I exclaimed. "Gee, that's great!"

"He's called Matey," Rula went on, happier now, "and he gets lost sometimes."

"And you've got a brother too, right?" I was really enjoying myself now.

"He's a boy," Rula said.

"Your brother?" I replied.

"No," she laughed, "Matey. All brothers are boys, worst luck."

I chuckled just like the Black Queen, and then retreated to the kitchen, where I laughed myself silly. After that, the rest was simple. I got out of my Black Queen costume and put everything away. I waited by the back door until I was quite sure Rula wasn't looking, until I knew the coast was clear. Then I let myself out, locked the house, slipped the key under the flower pot and ran down to the bottom of the garden. I scrambled up over the fence and let myself down behind the garden shed where no-one could see me. The last thing I saw was Rambo arching his back at me on the sundial and hissing hideously. "Same to you," I said, and went back home.

Chapter 6

Genius, Pure Genius

At supper Rula was full of it. "I wasn't frightened," she insisted, "not a bit. And she's not a witch at all. She's American and she's really nice."

"Well, she looks like a witch to me," I told her (I didn't want her spying on me again). "And if you know what's good for you," I went on, "you won't go snooping. She could turn you into a frog, or a slug maybe, or a worm. You'd make a good worm."

The television news was on and my father wanted to listen. "Can't you two do your squabbling somewhere else?" he snapped.

So Rula and I made ugly faces at
each other in silence instead. Matey sat
on the sofa between us, his nose
twitching.

"I bet he does it too," my father said.
He was leaning forward, watching the
television closely.

"What?" I asked. "Who?"

"Beats Purple."

"What's 'Purple'?" I had no idea what
he could be talking about.

"Purple's a computer, the best, the most sophisticated computer in the entire world, and the makers have challenged Greg McInley to a chess tournament. Just listen."

"Who's Greg . . . thingy?" Rula asked.

"World chess champion," I said, tutting at her and settling down to watch. "Don't you know anything?"

"Enough!" My father rounded furiously on us both. "Will you please shut up for a moment and let me listen."

There was a brief glimpse on the television of a young man getting out of a long black limousine and darting into a hotel. Then the reporter was talking to the camera. "McInley, world chess champion for the past five years, is still only twenty-three. Born in New York, he was a child prodigy – Grand Master at twelve years old – and now he's back here in New York to take up the 'Man Against Machine' challenge, against Purple, the most powerful computer yet devised. Man and machine will play one match a day, and it'll be the best of thirteen matches. If he wins, Greg McInley stands to win five million pounds. Not a penny, if he loses."

"He'll do it, you'll see," my father said. "I'm telling you, that man's a genius, a pure genius."

A shiver went right through me as I watched. I knew! At that moment I knew. You could say I put two and two together. Number 22 next door. The

Black Queen. Greg McInley was her son, he had to be. Hadn't she said he was nuts about chess, a "chess nut"? That was why there were chessboards everywhere. They were *his*, all *his*. And hadn't she said she was going to New York to be with her son, and for two weeks as well? It fitted. Everything fitted, fitted perfectly. That lady next door, Mrs Blume (a false name for sure), the Black Queen, was the mother of the world chess champion! She *had* to be.

It was all I could do to hold it in. I wanted to blurt it all out, tell everyone. But I knew I couldn't. I knew I mustn't. If I did that, I'd have had to tell the whole story, confess to everything, all the lies and the dressing up, all my play-acting.

The news came to an end, and my father turned off the television. "Well, Billy?" he said, turning to me. "That could be you in ten years' time, if you practise. Five million quid for a fortnight's work. Not bad. And he'll do it, I'm telling you he'll do it."

The next few days were not good, not good at all. I found it more and more difficult to find the right moment to sneak off and feed Rambo. It wasn't that anyone was suspicious, it was just that there was someone else in the house. Gran had come to stay with us in our new home for the first time, so that meant there was another pair of eyes I had to dodge. But somehow I managed to sneak away unseen each day, slip in

behind the garden shed and scramble
over into the Black Queen's garden.
Once inside her garden I felt safe
enough. But now every time I went into
Number 22 I was troubled by a terrible
temptation. I had this deep urge inside
me to sneak about the house looking for
evidence to confirm my theory about
her son. I longed to peek into one of the
front rooms, or even creep up the stairs
into the bedrooms. But I just didn't dare.

I was too frightened — frightened that someone might see me through a window; but more than that, I was frightened of the house. I didn't like being in there. It was dark and empty and cold — just like the haunted house of my dreams. Every time I went inside I just wanted to feed Rambo and get out as quickly as possible.

Feeding Rambo was never a problem. As soon as I was dressed up in the coat and floppy hat with the glasses on, he seemed to accept me totally as Mrs Blume, as the Black Queen. He loved me to bits. He'd even try to follow me back up the steps into the house. I had to shoo him away. I kept an eye out all the while for Rula. But I think I must have succeeded in frightening her off, for her face never again reappeared over the fence.

The news from New York was not good. Purple had won the first four matches. I kept thinking how disappointed the Black Queen must be, going all that way to New York just to watch her son lose.

Every time Greg McInley lost my father became more depressed. He'd read about it in the newspapers and come away miserable. "It's not like him, Billy," he'd say, "not like him at all. He keeps making mistakes, elementary mistakes. Greg McInley never makes mistakes." Then he'd blame Purple. "It's that lousy computer fazing him out somehow. He'll do better tomorrow, you'll see."

But tomorrow was always just as bad. Soon it was six matches to nil. If Greg McInley lost the next day, then that would be the end of it.

But the next day the real action moved from New York to back home. I was feeding Rambo late that afternoon when I saw Matey sitting in the long grass of Number 22, nibbling busily. He must have found another way through. Rambo hadn't even seen him – he was oblivious to everything except his food. I thought I'd act quickly before Rambo saw him, before someone came looking. I ran down the steps, picked up Matey, clambered up onto the rusty roller by the garden fence and looked over. Rula was just coming out into the garden, crying her eyes out and calling for Matey.

It was risky, but I was so into the part that I knew I could fool her. "Hey, kid," I called out. "You lost something?"

She stopped crying the moment she saw me and began to back away. "Matey," she said, "my rabbit. I can't find my rabbit."

I held up Matey by the scruff of his neck. "This what you're looking for?" I asked.

I could see she was still nervous of me, but all the same she came over, reached up and took him from me. I don't think she dared even look at me – which was just as well, I suppose.

"Thank you," she said, clutching him tight, and she ran off at once back into the house.

I was in the kitchen a few minutes later just taking off my floppy hat when I heard the bell ring, the front door bell. I stood there, hardly daring to breathe. The bell went again.

"Anyone home?" It was my mother! I heard Rula's voice too! Both of them were there. And Rula knew I was in that house, she'd only just seen me. I *had* to be there.

There was no way out. I had to say something. I made it up as I went along. "Listen," I called out. "It's a bit difficult. I'm washing my hair right now, OK?" I sounded just like her, the Black Queen, just like a woman, just like a real American.

"It's all right," my mother replied. "We didn't want to bother you. Rula and me, we just wanted to say thank you, that's all, for finding Rula's rabbit for us."

"No problem," I said.

"Maybe you'd like to come over sometime," my mother went on.

"That'd be fine," I said, "just fine. Thanks."

And then they were gone. I could not believe it. I had fooled my own mother. I was brilliant, utterly brilliant; but I was shaking like a leaf.

Chapter 7

Hide and Seek

The next day we heard that Greg McInley had beaten Purple for the first time, and once he'd started winning he didn't stop. Whenever the news came on breakfast television we'd be watching, all of us – Gran included, and she'd always said that chess was the most boring game there ever was.

Until now chess had been just a game for me – a game I enjoyed, but still just a game. Now it was becoming an

obsession. For me, for my own private
reasons, even more than for everyone
else in the house, the result of a chess
match between a man and a computer
had become more important than a
football World Cup final. Every day I
was aching to tell them who the Black
Queen was, that we had Greg McInley's
mother living next door to us. But I
could not bring myself to do it. It wasn't
that I was frightened of her any more –
she could hardly be a witch *and* Greg
McInley's mother, could she? But I had
promised her I'd say nothing and she
trusted me – she'd said so. And besides, I
knew that once I told them that, then I'd
have to tell them everything. I'd have an
awful lot to explain away. So I kept
quiet, but it was hard, so hard.

When, after five more wins, we heard
that Greg McInley had drawn level with
Purple at six matches each, we all went
berserk, leaping up and down like wild

things, so much so that Matey went and hid under the sofa.

Now it was on the television all the time, every news bulletin. And we weren't the only ones getting excited. Of course they only ever showed the last few moves of each match. Greg McInley would be sitting up there on a dimly lit stage, a great electronic chessboard behind him. He'd be hunched over the table like a concert pianist, his nose almost touching the chess pieces on the board. When he moved a piece he always did it in precisely the same way.

He'd sit back, brush his nose with his forefinger, then reach out very decisively. He'd tap the piece he was going to move three times, always three times, move it, punch the timeclock and sit back, then fold his arms and wait for Purple's move to come up on the electronic board.

When Greg McInley won there were no fists raised in the air in triumph, no smiles even. He'd just push his chair back and walk directly off the stage, completely ignoring the audience who'd be on their feet, clapping and cheering. I always looked for a glimpse of his mother in the audience. And I thought I did see her just once, a woman in black in the front row, but the camera passed by her so quickly that I couldn't be sure.

Evening after evening my father would take me through Greg McInley's most amazing moves, and he'd go on and on about the genius of the man to anyone who would listen. None of us could really understand the complexities of it. All we wanted to know was who was going to win. Man or machine? Greg McInley or Purple?

My father tried to stay up all night to hear the news of the last match – the deciding match – as it came in, but he fell asleep. So he didn't know the result any more than we did when it came on the breakfast news the next morning. We were all watching, watching and waiting. Then at last it came. "Chess. And Greg McInley has done it! Last night Greg McInley, world chess champion, beat Purple in the last match in the series. So he wins seven matches to six." Then we saw pictures of Greg McInley sitting up there on the stage in New York. We saw him sit back, stroke his nose, reach out, tap tap tap on the Black Queen and at last make his move. He punched the timeclock, and then came his voice, soft, deep, calm: "Checkmate." The cheering was thunderous. This time, when he stood up, he did bow just once, and I saw a flicker of a half smile, a shy smile on his face as he walked off.

The reporter went on: "That is

probably the last we shall see of McInley for some time. He will take away five million pounds in prize money, money which he usually gives away to good causes. An intensely private person, he never gives interviews. He will disappear, as he always does, into nowhere."

"Didn't I tell you?" cried my father. "Didn't I tell you?" He had tears in his eyes, and so did I, and so did Rula – but that was because she had lost Matey again. Matey turned up soon enough – my mother had shut him in the kitchen cupboard by mistake.

Later, when we were clearing up breakfast, Gran suddenly said: "No-one can disappear into nowhere. Someone must know where he goes. That chess man, he must have a family somewhere. Everyone has a mother." I felt myself going cold all over. "I mean," she went on, "someone must know where he goes to, surely to goodness."

"Listen, Gran," my father said, "if you've got a brain like he's got, you can disappear, just like that, easy as pie. That man can beat the best chess players in the world, the best minds and now the best machines. Do you really think he can't beat everyone at hide and seek too? If he doesn't want to be found, then I'm telling you, he *won't* be found."

"His mother would know," Gran said – she was not giving up the argument. "Find the mother – she'll know where he is."

I don't know why I said it. I heard the words come tumbling out of my mouth and could not stop them. "The Black Queen, at Number Twenty-two next door, maybe she's his mother," I began – everyone was gawping at me – "well, she could be. She's mad on chess. She's got chessboards all over her walls,

76

like pictures. I've seen them. Maybe she taught him. And she's American too, isn't she? Greg McInley's American, isn't he?" They were still gawping.

"You've been looking in at her windows!" my mother cried – she was furious. "You've been snooping!"

"I just looked, that's all. When I found Matey that time, I just had a quick look." I was in real trouble now.

"Well, you shouldn't have." Now my father was joining in too. "What if she'd seen you?"

"'She's away," I replied.

"She's not," Rula said. "I know she's not. I saw her yesterday through the fence. There's a hole. She was feeding her cat. It's a black one. It's called Rammy Rambo."

"You're not to do it again, Billy, you hear me?" My mother was simmering down, but she was still cross.

So was I. After all, I had tried to tell them. If they didn't believe me, then that was their fault. I stormed out in a huff. I needed to get out of the room anyway, to think things through. The more I thought about it now, the more I was convinced that the Black Queen had to be Greg McInley's mother. She'd be back soon enough. I'd ask her straight out.

That evening I waited until I was quite certain that Rula was safe in her bath before I went to feed Rambo. I discovered the little knotty hole in the fence she must have been looking through, and plugged it with earth – just to make her wonder. After I'd fed him Rambo just wouldn't leave me alone. He kept wrapping himself round my legs, badgering me for more food. I gave him some water – the milk had run out days ago – but he didn't seem to appreciate it at all. In the end I decided I would have to fetch him a little more food.

I was going back up the steps when I noticed I'd left the door open. Suddenly Rambo made a dash for it. He was up the steps ahead of me and in the house

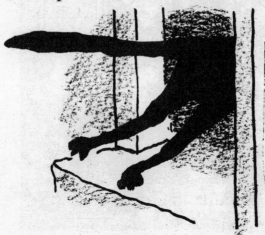

before I could stop him. He wasn't in the kitchen. He wasn't in the hallway. I called him and called him, but he wouldn't come. I tried tapping a bowl with a spoon. He still wouldn't come.

The Black Queen had told me I mustn't let him in. I had to find him and put him out, or he'd claw at the curtains and do messes. I went down the hallway towards the front door. The doors were all shut on either side. Rambo had to be upstairs.

I went after him. The stairs creaked horribly, every one of them. Something dark whipped across the window at the top of the stairs and screeched like an angry ghost. I could see it was only a branch, but every nerve in my body was jangling by now. The whole house felt alive all around me. I called out again, in a whisper this time. Still no Rambo. There were three doors leading off the landing. Only one was open, just ajar. He had to be in there. I pushed it open tentatively. Rambo was up on the bed, on the pillows, licking his paws and purring loudly. I was worried he might scratch me if I picked him up, so instead I tried to tempt him off the bed. He wouldn't budge. There were chessboards on the walls here too, and one with all the pieces set up on a table by the window. Then I noticed the framed photographs on the table. I knew I shouldn't, but I went over to look.

I was right! It *was* him! It was her son, Greg McInley, world chess champion — with the same shy smile on his face, holding a silver cup above his head. There was one of him standing on the porch of a house under snow, his arm around his mother — she had much longer black hair in those days and of course she looked a lot younger — and another of him as a boy proudly showing a medal and grinning happily through gappy teeth.

Suddenly Rambo was on his feet springing down off the bed. I soon saw why. In the door stood Mrs Blume, the Black Queen, Greg McInley's mother, and she did not looked pleased.

Chapter 8

Checkmate

"I was only looking," I said. She didn't look as if she believed me. "It was Rambo. He came upstairs. I couldn't stop him. Honest. He wouldn't come down."

She said nothing, but just looked at me, frowning. I was glad I wasn't having to lie, because I knew her eyes would find me out. Rambo was rubbing himself blissfully up against her leg, and I wondered how long it would be before he realized that two of us couldn't be the same person.

Still the Black Queen said nothing. I hated the silence, so I went on, "It's him, isn't it? In the photos. It's your son. It's Greg McInley. We've been watching. Everyone's been watching. All those chessboards, and you said he was a chess nut. And you told me you were going to New York to see your son. I guessed it all along. That's where you went, didn't you? He won. He beat Purple. My dad says he's a genius, a pure genius."

Suddenly her face softened, and she laughed. "It'll take more than some fool machine to beat my son," she said. I was so relieved to hear her speak, that she wasn't angry at me. She walked past me towards the window and looked out. "Good to be home. Hey, Billy, come see what I see." I went to look. "That's your bunny rabbit again in my backyard, isn't it?" she said. And sure enough there was Matey nibbling away at the grass by the sundial. "I reckon he likes the grazing better over my side of the fence."

That was when my hand accidentally knocked over one of the chess pieces –

the queen, the black queen. She stood it up again. "This was Greg's first chess set," she said. "He learnt all he knows on this board. Just a little old cardboard chessboard, cheapest one we could find down at the store. We had a lot of snow that winter, I remember. Too cold to go out. Nothing else to do but play chess. Only five at the time – took to it like a duck to water. We didn't know what we were starting, I guess we never do."

She still had her hand on the black queen. She tapped it three times, tap, tap, tap. Then she moved it.

"Checkmate," she said, her voice soft, deep, calm. She smiled down at me. Suddenly I knew. Suddenly I understood. It was a man's voice, *his* voice. I knew it too from the shy smile, from the tapping finger. It was difficult to take it in at first, just unbelievable. Unbelievable but true. She wasn't his mother at all; she was the *son*, she was him, she was Greg McInley, chess champion of the world. And she knew I knew. I could see it in her eyes, she could see it in mine.

Still smiling at me she took off her
glasses, and then her hat, then her wig.

"Sometimes, Billy," said Greg
McInley, "sometimes I reckon my mum
taught me too well that winter. The

pieces on this board, they became my family, my whole world. And now it's the only world I really understand, where I can be happy, where I can be myself. The other world out there, the real world, I don't want any part of it, not the money, not the fame, none of it. You understand me, Billy?"

I was beginning to.

"I never like to stay any place longer than a few months. Safer that way. And besides, I'm happy on my own. I play my chess, play my music. Bach — I could listen to his music all day and all night. It's all I need. I do it all in my mind, Billy. I've got a game of chess going on every board in this house, but up here in my mind. I play myself — that way I always win and I always lose, if you know what I mean. Do you know something, Billy? You're the first person I've ever wanted to tell. I reckon it's because you remind me of me when

I was young. Sometimes you want to share your secrets, you know what I mean? But you can only do it with someone you really trust."

He reached out and took off my hat and coat. "I guess you won't be needing these any more, will you?" he said. "Now, you'd best be getting that rabbit back home where he belongs, where you belong too."

We went downstairs together. "And thanks for looking after Rambo for me. Don't you worry, I'll be taking him with

me when I go. We can't have you
dressing up like a wicked old witch for
the rest of your life, can we now?"

"Are you going?" I asked.

"Better be moving on, Billy. I've been
in this place long enough, I reckon."

We said goodbye in the dark of the
hallway, and that was the last I saw of
him.

Matey was easy enough to catch. When
I got back Rula hadn't even realized he'd
gone missing. Then she clapped her hand
to her mouth and hooted with laughter
at me. "You're wearing glasses," she
screeched. And so I was. I said I'd found
them in the garden shed, and she
believed me.

No-one ever saw the Black Queen
again after that, or Rambo. Within days
a TO LET sign went up outside Number
22. Mrs Watson told Gran over the
fence that the Black Queen had gone,
that no-one had seen her going. My
father joked that maybe she'd just flown
away on her broomstick.

"She certainly was a strange one," my mother said. And that's what everyone thought. I "kept mum", as they say, and said nothing. It was our secret, Greg McInley's and mine; and besides, I knew they wouldn't believe me, not in a million years. Why should they? I had no proof.

A week later I answered the door to the postman. He had a parcel for us, he said. It was addressed to me. Somehow I knew at once that it was from *him*. I

took it up to my room to unwrap it in private. It was his cardboard chess set. "*For my good friend Billy, with love from Greg McInley (and Rambo).*" That was all it said, but it was enough. I was bursting to tell them. I came charging down the staircase and into the kitchen. I opened up the box and showed them. "That," I declared proudly, "is Greg McInley's chess set. He gave it to me."

They laughed at me, of course. So I showed them the letter, and then told them the whole crazy story. From beginning to end. No-one said a word the whole way through, and after I'd finished they just gawped.

THE END

LIZZIE ZIPMOUTH
Jacqueline Wilson

"**Why** don't you ever say anything, Lizzie?"
said Rory. "It's like you've got a zip across
your mouth."

Lizzie has zipped up her mouth. She doesn't
want to talk to Rory or Jake, her new step-
brothers, or Sam, their dad, or even her
mum. She's totally fed up at having to join a
new family and nothing can coax her into
speaking to them. Not football, not pizza,
not a new bedroom. That is, until she meets
a member of the new family who is even
more stubborn than her – and has had a lot
more practice!

A funny, touching story from the best-selling
author of *The Suitcase Kid*, *Bad Girls* and
Double Act. An ideal book for younger readers,
perfect for building reading confidence.

0 552 546534